GORDON

KU-001-517

Based on *The Railway Series* by the Rev. W. Awdry

Illustrations by
Robin Davies

EGMONT

EGMONT

We bring stories to life

First published in Great Britain 2004
This edition published 2007
by Egmont UK Limited
239 Kensington High Street, London W8 6SA
All Rights Reserved

Thomas the Tank Engine & Friends™

A BRITT ALLCROFT COMPANY PRODUCTION

Based on The Railway Series by The Reverend W Awdry
© 2007 Gullane (Thomas) LLC. A HIT Entertainment Company

Thomas the Tank Engine & Friends and Thomas & Friends are trademarks of Gullane (Thomas) Limited.
Thomas the Tank Engine & Friends and Design is Reg. US. Pat. & Tm. Off.

ISBN 978 1 4052 3202 9
1 3 5 7 9 10 8 6 4 2

Printed in China

All rights reserved. No part of this publication may be
reproduced, stored in a retrieval system, or transmitted,
in any form or by any means, electronic, mechanical,
photocopying, recording or otherwise, without the prior
permission of the publisher and copyright owner.

This is a story about Gordon the Big Engine. He was a very proud engine who always thought he knew best. But then one day something happened to make him realise otherwise . . .

Gordon was always boasting and telling the other engines how to behave.

One day, he was showing off to Edward.

"You watch me this afternoon as I rush through with the Express. That will be a splendid sight for you when you're shunting trucks."

And before he puffed away, Gordon said, "Don't play around with the trucks, Edward. It isn't wrong, but we just don't do it."

Edward ignored Gordon. It was fun playing with the trucks. He came up quietly behind them and gave them a push. Then he stopped suddenly and the silly trucks bumped into each other.

"Ooh!" they cried. "Whatever is happening?"

Edward played until there were no more trucks to move. Then he stopped to rest.

Suddenly, Edward heard a whistle. It was Gordon, and he was very cross.

Instead of pulling nice shiny coaches, he was pulling lots of dirty coal trucks!

"A Goods Train!" he grumbled. "The shame of it!"

Gordon went slowly past, with the trucks clattering behind him.

Edward laughed, and went to find more trucks.

But soon there was trouble. A Porter came and spoke to Edward's Driver.

"Gordon can't get up the hill," he said. "Will you take Edward to push him, please?"

Edward found Gordon halfway up the hill. His Driver was very cross with him.

"You are not trying!" he shouted at Gordon.

"I can't do it," replied Gordon. "The silly coal trucks are holding me back."

Edward came up behind Gordon's brake van, ready to push.

"You'll be no use at all," huffed Gordon.

"You wait and see," replied Edward.

The Guard blew his whistle and Gordon tried to pull forward as Edward pushed him as hard as he could.

"I can't do it, I can't do it, I can't do it," puffed Gordon.

"I will do it, I will do it, I will do it," puffed Edward.

Edward pushed and puffed with all his strength. And before long, Gordon was at the top of the hill.

"I've done it!" he said proudly, forgetting all about Edward, pushing behind. And Gordon ran on to the next station without stopping to say, "Thank You".

But The Fat Controller didn't forget to thank Edward. The next day, he was given a beautiful coat of blue paint with red stripes.

Gordon hadn't learnt his lesson. He still boasted and told the other engines how to behave. Now it was Henry's turn.

"Henry whistles too much," said Gordon. "Respectable engines don't whistle loudly at stations. It isn't wrong, but we just don't do it."

Poor Henry felt sad.

"Never mind," whispered Percy, "I like your whistling."

The next morning, as Gordon left the shed, he called to Henry.

"Goodbye Henry, be sure and remember what I said about whistling."

Later that day, Henry took a slow train to Edward's station.

"Hello, Henry," said Edward. "I was pleased to hear your happy whistle yesterday."

"Thank you, Edward," smiled Henry. "Shh! Can you hear something?"

Edward listened. Far away, but getting louder and louder, was the sound of an engine's whistle.

"It sounds like Gordon," said Edward. "But Gordon never whistles like that."

But it was Gordon. He came rushing down the hill at a tremendous speed. Gordon's whistle valve wouldn't close and he was whistling fit to burst.

He screamed through the station and disappeared.

"Well!" said Edward, looking at Henry.

"It isn't wrong, but we just don't do it," chuckled Henry, and Edward laughed.

Meanwhile, Gordon screeched along the line. People came out of their houses, fire engines set off to find the fire, and old ladies dropped their parcels in shock.

The noise was awful. Porters and passengers held their ears. The Fat Controller held his ears, too.

"Take him away," he bellowed. "And stop that noise!"

Still whistling, Gordon puffed sadly away.

He whistled as he crossed the points. He whistled in the siding. Gordon was still whistling as the last passenger left the station!

Then two Fitters climbed up and knocked Gordon's whistle valve into place. And at last there was silence.

Gordon slunk into the shed. He was very glad it was empty. He didn't want anyone to make fun of him.

Later that evening, the other engines came back.

"It isn't wrong," murmured Edward, "but we just don't do it."

And all the engines laughed, apart from Gordon.

From then on, Gordon was a much quieter, humbler engine – well for a few days, anyway!

Collect the other characters in the Thomas Audio range:

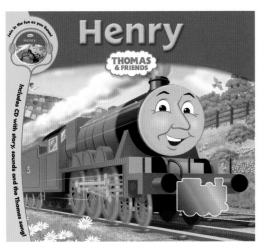

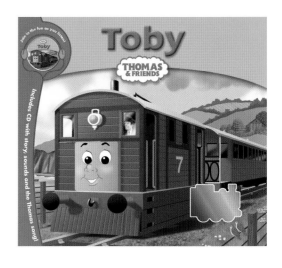